FREYA SLOANE

Green Bracelet

Contents

Content Warning

This is a very smutty/spicy novella with very little plot. This book contains Voyeurism, Free Use, and Exhibitionist. If that is not your vibe, please kindly exit this book.

Bracelet colors and their meanings:

- White - Virgin
- Red - No Touching/Unavailable
- Yellow - Ask
- Green - Free Use
- Rainbow - Lesbian/Gay

Chapter 1

Alyssa

How did I get here?

That's the question playing in my head as my back presses against a woman's body. But I already know the answer. I want—no, need—something more in my life. Something to get the blood flowing through me in ways I haven't felt… well, ever, really.

Every day feels the same. Work. Eat. Sleep. Boring. Mundane. Late-night doomscrolling led me to find this place. Sinful Desires. I practically stalked the site for months until I finally took the plunge and applied for a membership. It took two months for the approval to come through and another week before I finally set foot inside. But I did it. I'm here.

Sinful Desires is an exclusive sex club. The cost just to apply alone would make most people cry, not to mention the background check and physical that are required. Then there's the monthly fee.

Needless to say, I spent over a couple thousand.

I'm pretty sure when my grandmother left me money in her

will to do something fun, a this was not on the list. Though, if we are going to get technical, sex clubs are most definitely fun. At least I'm pretty sure they are. My aching pussy is screaming yes. Even if she has yet to be touched.

I'm not entirely sure how I ended up in this room, naked, and pressed against this woman.

That's another lie. I was enamored with everything the moment I stepped through the curtain, and I couldn't say no, couldn't pull myself away as she grabbed my hand and led me back here. Not to mention the colored band around my wrist signaled to everyone here that I'm free play. It would have been easy to pick red. Red said I was here to watch, observe, but I didn't want that. That's not why I joined. Plus, I was worried if I didn't dive right in, I might never. So headfirst I went.

Long, red nails slowly slide down my body, flicking over my pebbled nipples. My body heats at her touch. Her fingers trail lower and lower and I'm lost in a haze, lost in the burning of my core for more.

I'm not even sure of my own name but I do know I want her to touch me more. I want to touch her but she hasn't let me and I wonder if that's her kink. Denial. Watching whoever she's playing with squirm and pant for more.

Something deep inside of me, way down deep, doesn't want to be here. That part of me is terrified of what is happening as the woman's lips brush against my ear. I lean into her anyway, craving more.

"Such a good girl," she praises, touching me everywhere but where I want her touch the most.

There's a noise in the room, soft, barely noticeable, but fuck if I care. My entire body is humming with anticipation.

Her fingers glide along my outer thigh before she grips me

and spreads my legs apart, exposing my wet pussy to the cool air of the room. I groan from the exposure.

In front of me, I find a naked man. My gaze caught on his cock in his hand–the tip is dark purple and there's a drop of pre-cum leaking out–and the abs on his brown skin. I don't even care who he is, not that it would matter. A mask covers his face, and the unknown does something to me.

The man lowers, my eyes following the cock.

I could leave, I know I could. The woman is barely holding my legs open.

There are safety precautions in place, including the safe word I gave to the room guard. I could stop this, but I don't want to, not really. I'm here for this. Exactly this. To be used.

I'm soaked, aching, and I don't care that I'm not prepared for a cock. Let alone one of his size. Not to mention the moment his cock presses inside of me will be the first thing inside my pussy in weeks.

My pussy clamps around nothing at the thought.

It moves closer and closer until it's right up against my soaking cunt. Mouth open, I watch in awe as he presses his dick against my folds. He moves slowly. Painfully slowly. My pussy contracts, trying to suck the cock inside. The head finally vanishes inside of me and I fucking love the feel of this large cock spreading me. It burns in the most delicious way.

"Fuck," the man whispers. If it weren't for the quietness in the room, I wouldn't have heard it, and it does something to me. My heart rate rises and I stop breathing.

He continues to move slowly, sliding inside, and the moment he's all the way inside is the moment I finally let out a breath.

My eyes roll into the back of my head, and I let out a "fuck" as I lean my head against the woman's shoulder once again.

"Feels good, doesn't it, baby?" she asks, her lips skimming my neck, placing light kisses where she can reach as her fingers glide up and down my thighs.

I nod, opening my legs even more and raising my hips slightly. I need more. Want more. Crave more. "Please." I beg.

The man slides out slowly, and I whimper at the loss only to groan when he fills me back up.

He moves slowly in and out as hands roam my body, teasing my clit, pinching my nipples. Lips and tongues brush across my body. Hers. His.

I'm lost in the feeling. Unable to keep my eyes open as I enjoy everything being done to me, to my body. The way these two people oh so slowly bring me higher and higher and higher, not once letting me crash down into my orgasm.

"Please," I beg. My body is covered in a thin sheen of sweat. I'm not even sure how long we've been at this. How long my body has been used, touched, but I need to come. "Please, I can't… I can't take it anymore. I need… I need to come." They could deny me, continue their slow movements until they get what they want from me.

There's always my safe word, but I'm not ready. I need to see how far this can go, how far I can go. It can't be over. Not yet.

The man finally moves faster, harder. His body hovers over me, his breath fanning my face as he grunts.

The woman's fingers brush my sensitive clit, and I whimper as my legs shake.

"Are you going to come for me? For us?" she asks.

"Yes," I moan, feeling my pussy tighten around his cock.

"Open your eyes for me, baby. Open your eyes for me as you come all over his cock."

My eyes fly open, taking in the man hovering over me. His

hazel eyes are way too familiar, but I can't think about that. My orgasm slams into me, cutting off all thoughts that could run through my head, as I cry out. He slams his hips against me with a final groan as he comes, my pussy milking him of everything.

Chapter 2

Oliver

I shouldn't have done it. I shouldn't have removed the mask from my face. The shock and horror that flashed in her eyes before her orgasm overtook her told me as much.

But the minute she appeared from behind the curtain, the minute my eyes found her curvy, full body, her tight dress showing off every single curve and dip, all rationality went out the window.

I've wanted her for two years, watching her, learning as much as I could about her. But staying away. Alyssa was too good for me, too pure. The way her smile lit up a room, how her laughter was like heaven to my ears, the way her green eyes sparkled.

But as my eyes scanned her body and honed in on the green band on her wrist, I knew I had to scoop her up before anyone else did.

A quick nod to Nadia was all it took before she grabbed Alyssa and led her into a private room.

'Hammock' is her safe word, according to the man guarding the door. Each room has one—a guard. While there are rules in a place like this, sometimes—albeit rare—intervention is needed. In my two years here, it has only happened once that someone didn't stop even after the other participant yelled their safe word. They were immediately banned and put on a red list. The red list meant no other sex club would allow you to join. No matter how much money or "power" you had.

Alyssa looked beautiful lying on the couch with Nadia behind her, touching her. And the moment I stepped in front of them, Nadia spread Alyssa's legs, showing me just how wet this beautiful woman in front of me was. I was a goner.

Sliding into her wet, warm cunt did things to me I haven't felt ever, but the closer she got to her orgasm the more I needed her to know it was me bringing her this pleasure. It was my cock inside her pussy. My cock she was coming all over. So I ripped it off, tossed it on the floor, and made sure she opened her eyes when she came.

Now she's attempting to get dressed, muttering about how she can't believe any of this. But what I can't believe is how she really thinks I'm just going to let her leave.

No, she's mine now. Leaving isn't an option anymore. It can't be.

Nadia slips out the door, and I charge in front of Alyssa, stopping her from slipping her dress over those luscious hips as I push her against the wall.

Her eyes widen as she takes me in. Standing at six feet even, her head reaches my chest. Her mouth opens and closes, trying to find something to say but having no words.

"Do you have any idea what seeing you here did to me?" I ask her as I slide the tips of my fingers down her arm. "What seeing this green band on your wrist did to me?" I tug at the band. "This green band that means…"

"Free play," she whispers, finishing my sentence for me.

"Free play," I repeat. "You walk into my club, looking like a fucking dessert, wearing a band that tells everyone in here they can touch you, fuck you,"—her eyes dilate as I speak—"however they want, wherever they want." I tear the band off her wrist, letting it fall to the floor.

"Hayes," she whispers, calling me by my last name. It doesn't matter how many times in the last two years I have tried getting her to call me Oliver, she won't. "You can't—"

"Oh, but I did." My hand moves from her wrist to her round ass to the back of her thigh. She shifts her weight to her other foot, anticipating my next move. I left her leg, opening her up to me. "Because this"—I rub the tip of my still hard cock through her wet folds, our cum acting as lube—"is my cunt. My pussy." I slid inside her. Alyssa makes a noise in the back of her throat, and, fuck, I want to hear more of them. "You want a different cock inside my pussy, that's fine. But I decide when, not you."

I lift her other leg off the floor, holding her up as I slide the rest of the way inside, pressing her completely against the wall with my hips.

"Hayes," she moans, arching her back as she tries to ride my cock, but I'm in control here. Not her. Me.

"Are you mine, Alyssa?"

"That's not—"

I rotate my hips against her, cutting off her sentence with a moan. Her nails dig into my back, and, fuck, it feels fantastic.

"Hayes, please." She begs, trying and failing to fuck me.

I pull out until just the tip is inside her. "Tell me you're mine and I'll fuck this pussy."

"I'm yours. It's yours. You can have it. Please, just—" She gasps as I slam into her. I fuck her hard and fast. Enjoying the way her body moves against mine with every thrust. The way she feels soft and plump in my hands. The way her tits bounce.

She moans my last name, and I want to record it so I can play it on repeat. The sound of her moans is music to my ears.

She squeezes my cock as she comes, once again setting off my orgasm. I slam my lips to hers, drinking in her cries of pleasure.

Her thighs shake in my palms. "Arms around my neck, baby." I tell her, waiting for her arms to tighten around my neck before I pull us from the wall.

I sit back down on the couch we fucked on earlier with Nadia and hold her, soothe her, praise her. Aftercare—no matter what kind of sex you have with anyone—is the most important part. After making sure your woman comes first, of course.

Once her heart rate calms and her breathing returns to normal, I finally allow her to pull away from me.

"I should go," she says, climbing out of my lap before I can stop her.

"Alyssa," I say in a lame attempt to stop her.

She pulls her dress down over her hips and moves to where her heels are lying on the floor.

"We should talk about this." I stand trying to stop her, but she's already at the door, and I'm tugging my pants through one leg.

"See you at work, Hayes." I'm stuck standing there, one pant leg up, the other stuck, staring at the door she just walked out of.

"Fuck," I curse, let my pants drop to the floor and wonder what the fuck just happened.

Chapter 3

Alyssa

I am one hundred percent, without a doubt, an idiot. But what Hayes did… He knew who I was from the beginning. I didn't wear a mask to hide my identity. And sure, I knew going in there was a possibility I'd run into someone I know; I'm not naïve enough to think everyone I know is vanilla. But the fact that he saw me and then hid who he was, only to reveal it at the end. That was just all kinds of wrong.

Maybe I should have stayed and had that conversation with him he seemed to have wanted, but I couldn't. Terrified doesn't even begin to cover what I was feeling—still am feeling. Clearly, he wanted me. But to what capacity?

I was at Sinful Desires to explore myself, my wants, my needs. What Hayes said, what he got me to say, isn't why I joined.

I ache to let my darkest desires come to fruition. And that's what the club was supposed to be. A way to let my hair down, to be wanted, used for someone else's pleasure.

It's something I've only dreamed about, allowing myself to fantasize about late at night.

Explaining to a partner that you basically want your body to be used by anyone and everyone is not something you talk about over dinner. And in my experience, when I've tried dipping my toe in that kind of conversation, I was quickly reminded just how boiling hot the water is. Most men want monogamy, and while I'm fine with that, I also desire more occasionally.

I don't want planned partners. I want to lie out on a table, in a room full of people, naked with my legs spread, and let myself be used, however and for however long.

Hayes wanted to give his permission, wanted to own me. My body. My pussy.

Someone touches my arm, and I'm brought back to the present. Haylie is looking at me with concern in her eyes. "Are you okay? You, like, zoned out for a good ten minutes."

I look around the arena, realizing I'm supposed to be at work snapping pictures while the players practice for tonight's game. It's a big one; we are going up against our biggest rival.

"Yeah, sorry. Just…" I shake my head. "I'm fine."

Haylie stares at me, and I know she doesn't believe me. But what am I supposed to say? 'Sorry, I got lost in the fact that I fucked one of the players after I signed up to join a sex club where I can wear a bracelet that tells everyone they can do whatever they want to me.' Yeah, I think not.

"Okay, if you're sure."

There's concern in her voice, but I nod, ignoring it, and look back towards the ice. The players are walking off toward the locker room. Looks like practice is over.

I shut my camera off and stand. "See you in a few hours, Haylie."

"Yeah, see ya," she says as I walk away. As much as I know Haylie is worried, this isn't something I'm comfortable talking about right now. Hell, maybe never. For now, I just need to keep my head on straight and keep moving. Even if it is insanely difficult.

***

I sit on the floor in the arrival hallway. Players will arrive any minute, and I'm panicking internally. I've done everything I can to avoid Hayes the last few days, but I can't stay away anymore. I tug at my oversized sweater, making sure it hides the rolls my stomach is no doubt making as I sit here.

I'm not ashamed of my size; in fact, I love my body, but right now I don't want to be in it, and it's all his fault.

The doors open and two players walk in, giving a smile and a wave as I snap their pictures. It doesn't take long for me to get lost in my job.

I'm laughing at something a player, Thorton, says when the air in the hallway changes. He's here.

Thorton walks off, and I turn around to snap his picture, do my job. But the moment I raise the camera up and look through the viewfinder, I stop breathing. His gaze is on mine, and he is anything but happy. I snap a picture, capturing the anger on his face, before lowering the camera. His eyes don't leave mine as he passes, and I swear I can see what he's saying to me. How dare I allow Thorton to make me laugh.

It sends a ripple of pleasure straight to my pussy. Why? I'm unsure. My desire isn't ownership, and yet my thighs tighten together as I try to get this ache under control. Hayes sees it, my slight movement, and his eyes turn from anger to hunger.

Someone screams in excitement, and I break away from his gaze, looking back towards the entrance.

I attempt a few pictures of the player that just walked in, but I can barely focus. Not until Hayes is through the locker room door.

"What was that?" Haylie asks me once all the players have arrived and we are walking towards the arena for game photos.

"What was what?" I ask, feigning confusion as I mess with my camera settings and change out the lens.

"That look Hayes gave you? He looked pissed. What did you do?"

I shake my head. "No, he didn't. And even if he was mad, why do you think he's mad at me?"

She puts her hands on her hips, her camera dangling from the strap around her neck. "Uh, maybe because when he first walked through the door he was smiling and then he…" Her eyes widen as she gasps. "Oh em gee, he likes you!" she practically screams.

I shake my head. "No, that's not—"

She hits me on the arm. "He totally does. He got pissed off when he saw you laughing at Thorton. He totally has a crush on you."

I roll my eyes, ignoring the thumping in my chest that is my heart. "Haylie, you are seeing things."

"Yeah, clearly through a camera lens." She picks up her camera, gives a little shake.

I take a test shot to make sure I'm happy with my settings and needing something to do.

"Look," she says as she nudges me to get me to look over at her camera screen. "This is Hayes when he first walked in." There's an enormous grin on his face as he walks through the door. "And this," she changes the image twice before stopping, "is Hayes when he sees you laughing with Thorton." The anger on his face is undeniable. Tight lips, slanted eyes, jaw tight. It's the exact face he had when I finally snapped his picture, only he's looking at my camera in mine. Well, he's looking at me if we want to get technical.

"That proves nothing," I say, feigning indifference.

Haylie scoffs. "Yeah right. Deny it all you want, but that man wants you badly, girl. Like real bad."

"Whatever. We need to get to our spots before they come out of the tunnel."

I'm walking away when she yells out, "Ignore it all you want, Alyssa. But that man wants to dick you down, and you should totally go for it!"

A blush rises to my face as the people around us turn and stare. I can't believe she yelled that out with people around.

But I can't imagine what she would say if she knew he already did. Twice.

It doesn't take me long to get to the area of the rink I'm in charge of. But it takes a few more minutes to push the thoughts of Hayes and what happened in that room of the club far from my mind. I'm here for one thing and one thing only. To take pictures of a hockey game. It's my job, and if I can't focus enough to snap the pictures for the social media department, I'll feel like a failure.

Hayes, and his body, and that anger on his face will just have to wait. Hopefully forever.

Chapter 4

Oliver

When it comes to Alyssa, I have always had issues. Every smile, every laugh that wasn't directed towards me made me feel things. I wanted them, all of them. They just weren't mine to take. But things are different now. I've had her. Had a taste. Felt the way her pussy wraps around my cock as she comes. The sounds she makes as I fuck her. Now I'm a man possessed.

She's been avoiding me for days, and I've spent the last three nights at Sinful waiting for her to show up. But she never did.

I'm determined to get her to talk to me. We need to talk. And the longer I go without seeing her, the more upset I get.

She's avoiding me, and I can't fucking stand it. And to make matters worse, as I walked inside and saw her laughing with fucking Thorton, I wanted to pummel his fucking head into the wall. Screw the fact that he's a teammate. He made her laugh; they spoke.

They spoke, and she's ignoring me.

I skate on the ice, waiting for the game to start. She wasn't around during warm-ups, and I'm not sure I'm ready to see if she's still missing, so I keep my head down and try to get my thoughts straight before the puck drops.

Hockey is important to me, and I can't let things that are happening off the ice affect me on the ice.

The puck drops, and the game is on. I skate down the ice, keeping my eye on the puck. It's currently in Kaprizov's possession, then Oliander has it and he passes it to me. I take it down the ice before passing back to Kaprizov. A flash of blue catches my eye, and before I can stop myself, I look. Alyssa is standing in her spot, her camera up to her eye as she snaps away. She's here.

I mean, of course she's here; it's her job. But I didn't allow myself to think she would be there. I figured after what happened earlier she would have left.

Someone nudges me, and I look at him.

"Head in the fucking game, Hayes," Kolesnik, our team captain, says before skating away chasing after the puck.

Right. The game.

I try my best, but by the end of the first period, I have made so many mistakes I'm sure Coach is about to bench me.

"What's the problem, Hayes?" Kolesnik asks.

I shake my head before squirting water into my mouth. "Nothing."

"Well, it doesn't seem like nothing. If you can't figure it out in the next few minutes, you'll be pulled from the game. Get it together. Now."

We get back on the ice, but my head still isn't right. It probably won't be until I can talk to Alyssa.

Kolesnik gives me a look that tells me he's about to pull me, and I wouldn't blame him. My fuck up allowed our biggest rival to get a goal.

I slid up to the Plexiglass in front of Alyssa and bang my fist. She jumps at the sudden impact and turns to me, wide-eyed.

"What the fuck are you doing, Hayes?" Alyssa and Oliander ask at the same time.

Ignoring Oliander, I keep my eyes on Alyssa. "Meet me at Puck Side after the game."

"What?"

"Meet me. At Puck Side. After the game."

Her jaw drops, but she recovers quickly. "Are you crazy, Hayes? The game is going."

"Hayes, what the fuck are you doing? Get your ass back in the game," Coach screams at me from the players' bench, but I'm ignoring everyone, even the referees.

"Agree to meet me."

She's staring at me wide-eyed.

Someone tugs on my sleeve, but I ignore them, my focus on the woman in front of me.

"Okay," she says.

"What was that?" I ask, wanting to hear the whole thing.

"Okay. I'll meet you at Puck Side."

"After the game," I clarify. The arena is getting louder as I stand here. I can't play correctly until she agrees, until I know she's going to talk to me. Tonight.

"Yes, after the game. Now go play before they sideline you."

A large grin spreads on my face as she agrees, her cheeks pinking up from being embarrassed by the show I created between us. But I don't care because she agreed, and I'm going to get what I want. Her.

***

After spending some time in the sin bin for delay of game, I feel lighter, faster on the ice, and we win the game. 3-2.

"Hayes!" Coach screams my name as we walk inside the locker rooms after the game. "Your ass, my office, now."

I barely even have my skates off, so I slip my shoes on and head towards Coaches' office.

"You want to explain what the hell that was out there?"

I take a moment and wonder how to answer, but can't come up with something that doesn't sound completely unreasonable and maybe slightly insane. "Not really. No."

He stares at me, clearly trying to figure out how to respond. After a few minutes he shakes his head and waves his hand at me. "Get the fuck out of my office, Hayes, and if you ever do something like that again, consider yourself benched for the rest of the season."

I don't respond, just walk out the door and hit the bike for a cool down then the showers before meeting my woman at Puck Side.

***

Puck Side is more packed than usual as I make my way inside. No thanks to me, I'm sure. Everyone wants to see what could possibly be going on between me and the camera girl.

My eyes scan the bar until they finally land on her, hiding in the corner. I get slapped on the shoulder and congratulated as I make my way over to her but I barely respond to anyone, too focused on the woman trying to hide near the back of the bar.

She stares at me as I approach, and I hate that I'm unsure what the look on her face means.

"Out of all the places you could possibly get us to meet at. You have to pick the most public one." There's an edge to her voice, a mix of humor and annoyance.

I shrug a shoulder, moving closer to her. "Pretty sure asking you to meet me at Sin was the last thing either of us wanted."

I watch as her cheeks turn pink, sure her chest is sporting the same color, but it's hidden beneath her team hoodie. If I turned her around, would my name be on the back? If not, I really need to fix that.

"Right," she whispers.

"So, about the other day…"

Chapter 5

Alyssa

"So about the other day…"

My face feels hotter as I think about what we did three days ago. The memories go straight to my pussy and, fuck, I'm wet. It should matter that Hayes tried to claim me all for himself, but it doesn't. He did exactly what I wanted, used my body for his pleasure. Even if I did come both times. My own pleasure doesn't matter when I think about being used. Me getting off is just a bonus. Plus, I'm used to horrible sex where I don't find a release until I'm alone.

"There's nothing to talk about. I joined for a specific reason, and tying myself to one person isn't what I'm looking for."

He leans closer to me, his lips brushing against my ear as he speaks. "Even if it gets you exactly what that pretty pink pussy of yours wants. To be used by multiple people back to back to back."

A shiver runs down my spine, and I squeeze my thighs together, trying to find some type of relief. But the image in my head of being spread out while I'm being filled as Hayes watches from the side is doing things to me. Things I'm not sure I even wanted.

My fingers grip his hoodie, and a whimper escapes my throat.

"Does that turn you on, baby? If I slid my fingers inside you, would I find you soaked?"

I lean forward, my forehead pressing against his chest. "Hayes," I practically moan.

Why was he doing this? Asking me this? Is that even his kink? I don't even know why he goes to Sinful Desires. Is he a voyeur? Maybe a dom? He did want to own and control me.

"Talk to me, Alyssa. Tell me what's going through that pretty head of yours."

A glass shatters somewhere, bringing me back to the fact that we are having this conversation in a room full of people at a fucking hockey bar of all places. People who are, more than likely, watching us curiously. It shouldn't, I know it shouldn't, but that fact only turns me on even more.

Any of the people surrounding us could overhear, could know exactly what it is we are discussing.

"We shouldn't…" The sentence dies on my tongue. Clearly, Hayes picked this place for a reason. He knew the conversation we would have here.

I stare down at the outline of his cock through his pants. He's hard, and even though I shouldn't, I let the hand gripping his hoodie slide down and brush my fingers against him. He groans at the motion.

"Alyssa…" My name is a threat, only I don't know what kind, and the thought of finding out sends a thrill down my spine.

I open my hand and press my palm against him.

"Fucking hell," he curses. "Meet me in the back. Five minutes."

He barely gives me enough time to agree before he steps away and vanishes.

My heart is racing in my chest, and my breathing has quickened as I think about what we are about to do with so many people around. Would they hear us? Probably not, but the possibility has me walking towards the back before the five minutes are even up.

A door opens and I'm pulled inside a room. I barely have time to look around—it's a storage closet—before Hayes is pushing my back against the door.

He hooks his fingers inside my jeans and yanks them, and my panties, down. A thrill runs through me again as he turns me around and presses the top of my back until I'm leaning over, my bottoms bunched at my ankles.

He slams his cock inside me. My walls tighten around him at the sudden intrusion as I gasp.

"Unless you want everyone to know what I'm doing to you inside this closet, I suggest you keep quiet."

I bit my bottom lip to stifle my whimper, and the thought of people knowing what is happening in this closet makes me wetter. It shouldn't; it's wrong on so many levels. The main one being that no one on the other side of the door has agreed to hear us. We are in public for fuck's sake.

Hayes slides out and in. "Fuck, baby. Does that turn you on?"

He keeps moving, his fingers gripping my hips. It's quick, fast, and I can hear how wet I am. I try to find something to grab onto, only finding my own clothing, but, fuck, holding back my moans and cries is brutal. About as brutal as Hayes is being while he fucks me raw.

He slams into me hard, grunting as his cum coats my walls. My pussy throbs with the need for a release.

I whimper as he pulls out. He helps me stand, and I realize

he's already put his dick back in his pants.

"Sinful Desire. Wednesday night, seven. Don't be late." With that, he walks out the door, leaving me standing there with his cum leaking from my pussy and my pants still around my ankles. He used me for his own pleasure. I didn't even come. My thighs squeeze and rub together, feeling his cum leak out of me. My thighs slick with his release. I will think about this moment for the next few days. Using it to get myself off until Wednesday.

That was his plan all along. Find a way to tempt me into showing up, and damn it, it's going to work.

Chapter 6

Oliver

Leaving Alyssa in the closet was difficult. Seeing her face flushed, her pupils dilated in lust and desire, my cum dripping from her pussy had me struggling to leave. But I did it. I wanted her on edge, curious about what Wednesday would bring, so she would show up.

I was a man with a plan, and I was going to stick with it. Even if it did leave me with an unfinished feeling.

Wednesday night finally rolls around, and I'm sitting at the bar at Sinful Desires waiting for Alyssa to show up. I ordered a whiskey–the club has a one drink rule–but have yet to take a sip. I'm too excited about tonight. Coming here early was a mistake. Only because waiting is driving me mad. My leg bounces up and down as I roll the glass in my hand and glance at the entrance every two seconds.

The moment Alyssa walks through the curtains, my breath leaves my lungs, and I swear my heart stops beating. She looks… Incredible. The way her red shirt stretches over her tits, the low V showing them off, her short black skirt just covers her pussy and ass, and the high stiletto heels have me holding back a groan.

She's wearing a green bracelet around her wrist, and my cock strains against the zipper of my slacks, just begging to be inside of her.

Her eyes scan the room, and as she spots me, a small blush forms on her face along with a slight smile.

She carefully walks over to me, and I keep my gaze on her because if I look around the room and see all the men staring, wanting a taste of her, I'm not sure how I will react. Murder, probably. Fighting, absolutely.

The moment she reaches me, I wrap a possessive arm around her waist, pulling her in between my legs.

"Hi," she says, her voice breathy, and I swear I can smell her arousal as much as I can hear it.

"Hi," I answer back. "Glad you showed up."

She lowers her head, bringing her lower lip between her teeth before she replies, "Curiosity."

I hum and the moment her eyes meet mine again, I'm tempted to throw her over my shoulder and keep her for myself. But I know that's not what she wants. And I'd be a liar if I didn't want to see her fantasy come to life.

I want to watch her be fucked over and over by different people. I want them to know what it feels like when her pussy has their cock in a vice grip. Know what sounds come from her throat as they touch her, fuck her, make her come.

"Are you ready to know what I have planned?"

She nods. "Yes." It's soft, hungry. She's ready and so am I.

"There's a room on the second floor, and I think you will fit right in there."

She nods, but I can see the excitement in her eyes.

"There will be men and women who would be so excited to get a piece of you in there."

"And you'll be there?"

"I will be. But you won't know where. There are some areas in the room that are dark, where I can sit and watch. But there are also two-way mirrors. I'll be… somewhere." I tease. I plan on utilizing both. Watching from the mirrors for a bit until slipping into the room. "But with your green bracelet, you'll get exactly what you want, Alyssa."

Her thighs rub together, and I know she's imagining it. Imagining all the things that could be done to her.

"Can we go now?" She asks, the excitement leaking from her voice.

"Of course." I say, grabbing her hand and pulling her towards the elevator, leaving my untouched drink behind.

Chapter 7

Alyssa

Hayes leads me into the elevator and—once on the second floor—down a hallway till he stops in front of a door. He pulls a red bracelet from the pocket of his jeans and tucks it inside my bra, his fingers brushing my nipple. A gasp leaves my lips at the contact made, and I swear I'm on the verge of coming right outside that room.

I've been wet all fucking day. For the last few days, if I'm being honest. The moment Hayes left me in that closet with promises of today, it's all I thought about. I'm pretty sure my co-workers think something is wrong with me. Between daydreaming during meetings and barely making deadlines the last three days, I look like I've lost my mind.

"When you're done, you can slip it on and I'll come to you. Otherwise, I'll seek you out when I'm ready and put it on you myself. Understand?"

I nod, my throat and mouth too dry to give a verbal response.

"Whenever you are ready, walk inside."

He takes a step away from me before he moves forward again

and slams his lips to mine in a quick kiss. I don't even have time to react before he's pulling away and disappearing into the room next door.

I take a deep breath and then enter.

On the other side of the door is a small room and a guard. He gives me a once-over before nodding and opening the other door for me.

Walking through the door is like walking into a whole other world. Men and women, some in various stages of sex and undress, are inside. The room looks like a similar version of the area downstairs, only smaller. Couches and chairs are spread sporadically, with a small bar in the middle of the room. Men walk around naked, their cocks covered in condoms for safety reasons, and the thought that one of them could be inside me soon only makes the situation happening in my nether regions worse.

I scan the room, wondering where to go first. Would it be better to sit at the bar, on a couch, a chair?

Eventually, I settle on the bar. As I make my way over there, I'm stopped, thrown over the edge of the closest couch, and someone's cock slams inside of me.

The whole thing knocks the air from my lungs and it isn't until the guys third thrust that a sound finally comes from my throat.

I want to turn around, see who's fucking me but I'm stuck, unable to move even an inch and fuck does it feel like heaven. With every thrust of his hips, I'm sent higher and higher, but before my orgasm can happen, he stills inside of me and grunts his own release.

"Fuck, your pussy was tight." He says, his voice gruff.

He pulls out of me and I stay there with my legs spread, pussy throbbing and practically dripping as I catch my breath.

I've barely even begun catching my breath before someone else's cock is sliding inside of me.

Fuck, this feels good.

Chapter 8

Oliver

Watching Alyssa get fucked by different men, and her pussy eaten by a woman, has me feeling some type of way. It's not jealousy, far from it. It's a huge turn-on, knowing she's getting exactly what she wants—her pussy used over and over again. Being able to watch is more of a turn-on than I thought it would be.

Before her first time walking in here, I thought if I ever had a taste, I'd want to keep her all to myself, and I did. At first. But seeing the way her face lit up at the thought of being used did the opposite. I wanted it. Wanted to see it.

Watching other people fuck has always been a turn-on for me, but I never once imagined I'd be into watching the woman I want in my bed fuck other people. I thought we would watch people fuck together.

I've been watching closely. Well, as closely as one can from across the room, but I can see the blissed out look on her face. She loves this, and it's making my cock ache to be inside her.

I decided on a number earlier. The number of men who get

to fuck and use her pussy. Five.

I may not know her sexual history, but I know she's new to this, new to being used for someone else's pleasure, and I don't want it to become overstimulating. The first few times in here can be tricky for a newbie, and while the guards are great at seeing people reach their limits without themselves being aware, that is the last thing I want for Alyssa.

My steps are slow as I walk over to where Alyssa is currently lying on a table. Her skirt bunched around her stomach, her legs still spread even as the guy walks away. There's a sheen of sweat covering her body as her chest rises and falls with every breath she takes.

"Hey, baby." I whisper as I stand near her head. Her eyes pop open at the sound of my voice, and she smiles as she takes me in.

"Hayes," she practically sings my name. "Are you stopping me already?" she asks, her voice light and airy. "I want to come more. Need it."

I carefully reach inside her shirt, pulling out the red bracelet and slipping it gently on her wrist.

"Are you going to help me with that?" She asks as I move her around so I can lift and carry her out of the room.

She leans her head against my collarbone, nuzzling her face as she hums.

As much as I, and my cock, would love to slip inside her, she seems worn out. I'm not in a place to abuse the trust she has in me. My plan is to get her in a bath and assess her headspace. After that, maybe I'll slip inside her, and we'll both get the release we desperately need.

I key in the code to the room I booked for her aftercare and head straight for the bed. Setting her down and watching as she curls up into a ball and hums. Once she seems comfortable enough, I walk into the attached bathroom and start filling up the large tub with warm water. I strip off my clothes before walking back into the room and strip Alyssa of hers so we can slide inside the warm water.

Alyssa hums, pressing her back against me as much as possible once the water covers us.

The goal here isn't to clean her but to help her relax and recover, but she's currently making those things very difficult since she keeps grinding her ass against my aching erection.

"Alyssa, what are you doing?" I ask, knowing full well what she's doing.

"Hoping you'll solve both our problems." She answers with a giggle.

"Alyssa," I warn through tightened teeth.

She turns around in the tub, her eyes bright and filled with lust and need as she presses her pussy against my length. "Please, Hayes. I feel like I might combust if I don't come. I was so close, and it would be so much better if you did it with me." She pouts. "Don't make me do it on my own."

"I don't want to overwhelm you. You've experienced a lot tonight. Just want to make sure your head is okay." I whisper, palming the side of her face.

"My head is just fine. But my pussy isn't; she needs a release, Hayes. Now."

My eyebrows raise at the demanding way she says 'now'. "Is that how you think you'll get what you want? By demanding it."

She shrugs. "I guess I could always just take it."

Note to self: Alyssa turns into a brat when she's feeling needy. Instead of trying to hold her off, I grip her by her hips and then slam her down on top of me. Her pussy wraps so tightly around my cock I almost come on contact.

Alyssa practically screams as I move her up and down my cock hard and fast, water sloshing out of the tub as I move her.

"Ha-yes" she moans, throwing her head back.

"Look at me," I demand. "Fucking look at me, Alyssa."

Her head snaps back, her eyes meeting mine, and her mouth drops open. I want to kiss her, slam my lips onto hers and taste her mouth, but her pussy is choking my cock as her orgasm slams into her, stealing the sounds from her lungs and my release from me. I swear I black out.

She collapses against me, even as her pussy continues to pulse around my still-coming cock.

I'm still hard inside her, but I can't move, not yet. There is no telling just how sensitive we both are and moving now could be too much.

My fingers lightly trail up and down Alyssa's spine as she breathes, and it's as I notice her sniffling that my motions stop and my entire body freezes.

"Alyssa?"

She shakes her head, wrapping her arms around my neck and pulling me closer as I try to look at her.

"Talk to me, baby. Tell me what's wrong?" I'm freaking out. My mind races with so many thoughts. Did I hurt her? Does she regret what happened just now, or in the free use room? Is she okay?

"I don't know," she chokes out. "It was so good. Felt so good. But I can't—" she sobs, her grip on me tightening.

I let out a small breath as I hold her tightly, running my hand up and down her back as I soothe and shush her. "It's okay, baby. You're okay, Alyssa. You've been through a lot, felt a lot in the last few hours. I'm here. I'm right here, and I'm not going anywhere." I continue to comfort her, whisper sweet nothings and tell her she's going to be okay, and I'm not leaving her.

It's unsure how long we stay in the tub of cold water, but I don't dare move us until her sobs stop and her breathing evens out.

Chapter 9

Alyssa

Nothing beats the embarrassment I feel after the events that unfolded a week ago, not even the first time. I'm so embarrassed that I have done everything I can to ignore and avoid Hayes as much as my job will allow. Including passing on two jobs to a co-worker that I probably shouldn't have handed over. But it's too late now, and I can tell by the look on my boss's face that she is furious with me.

"Do you know why I asked you to cover kids' night, Alyssa?" She doesn't even give me a chance to reply before saying, "Because I like you. Because you are fantastic at getting the right pictures and angles we need for our social media team and the team's website. Why did you pass it off to someone else?"

Because I embarrassed myself in front of one of the hockey players by sobbing after he gave me an amazing orgasm after being fucked and used by a couple men and one woman.

Yeah. Can't say that, can I?

"I'm sorry, Mrs. James. It won't happen again," is the reply I go for.

While I'm unsure what the fraternization rules are between players and photographers, I don't intend on finding out. What happens at Sinful Desires isn't anyone's business. And sure, we also fucked at Puck Side, but that was a fluke, a moment of insanity that will never happen again.

"Be sure that it doesn't, Alyssa." She turns on her four-inch heels and walks away, making me feel like complete shit.

"You okay?" Haylie asks as she stands beside me, watching our boss walk away.

My shoulders slump. "No." Turning to look at her, I debate on what to tell her, if I should tell her anything.

Haylie is the closest person I have to a friend since I moved here. I'm too wrapped up in my job to have made any friends, but I need someone to talk to about what is happening. I just don't know what all I can tell her.

"What are your views on sex?" I ask.

Haylie's eyes widen as she looks at me before laughing. I stand there, waiting for her to finish.

"I'm sorry." She says, trying to stop, but every so often a giggle escapes her mouth. "That was very blunt." She clears her throat, a hand on her chest as she takes a few deep breaths. "I mean, we all have our kinks or whatever. Why?"

"Have you heard of Sinful Desires?"

Haylie tilts her head to the side. "The sex club? Obviously."

I bite my lip, debating whether I want to tell her, but I decide to go for broke. "I'm a member."

Her jaw drops. "But the membership is—"

"That's not important. I had some savings. But I may have… run into someone that works here while there and…" I trail off, not wanting to explicitly come out and say it.

Her forehead crinkles and her mouth turns down. "I don't understand, Alyssa. Isn't that the point of the club?"

"Yes but I…" I run a hand down my face with a groan. "I completely embarrassed myself the other day with him. Which is why I kept giving my work to others."

She nods. "Because you can't face him." Her eyes widen as she gasps. "Oh em gee. Who was it?" She moves closer and whispers, "Was it the boss? Someone in the photography department?" She grips my arm as she gasps again. "Was it a player?"

Something on my face must have given me away because she practically squeals in excitement. "It was a player, wasn't it?" Her voice is low but I still want to shush her as my face turns red. "Oh em gee, was it Hayes? It was Hayes, wasn't it? That's why he was acting all weird at the game two weeks ago when he wouldn't leave you alone. Alyssa!" She grips my arms and shakes me as she jumps in place and squeals. At least the hallway is empty. The last thing I need is anyone looking our way and making me feel even more embarrassed than I already do.

"Tell me it's Hayes," she asks as she calms down.

"I can't confirm or deny anything." My contract forbids it. Outing anyone who visits the club could get my membership voided along with a hefty fee. Even if I could talk about it, admit it was him, I'm not sure I could actually do it. It isn't my place to tell anyone anything about his sex life and the things he likes. Admitting that he's a member feels like an invasion of privacy, and this is all technically speculation to Haylie. Without a membership herself or me outright admitting it, she doesn't really know. Right?

She squeals and jumps up and down yet again, but suddenly she stops. "Wait. So then…" she stares at me as she tries to put the pieces together. "I'm confused."

I can't admit out loud that I sobbed in his arms after what I'm sure was, and will be, the greatest orgasm of my life. "I just embarrassed myself and now I can't face…that person."

"But you work together. Kind of. I mean, you'll see him tonight. It's a home game."

I groan. "I know." The team has been playing away games for four games, but tonight they are back home, which means I'm back to photographing the players' entrances and the game itself. That's the one good thing about still being a lower man on the totem pole: I don't have to follow the team to their away games.

"It'll be okay, Alyssa. I'm sure Hayes doesn't even care that you embarrassed yourself. It's probably already forgotten, anyway." She threads her arm through mine and pulls me beside her so we can get our cameras and whatever else we need to do our jobs and try as I might to forget about what happened in that tub, I can't.

It's going to be a long night.

Chapter 10

Oliver

Alyssa has been avoiding me; I know it. Ever since she broke down in the tub last week I haven't seen her. At least not really. I caught a glimpse before we left for our away games, but she wasn't at Kids' Night, and I was hoping I could get a moment alone with her then.

I tried to talk to her in the room that night when she finally calmed down, but she shut me out, got dressed, and left before I could even tug my own pants on. Again. It pissed me off then and it pisses me off now. Especially because I still don't have her phone number. Not that I think she'd answer a call or respond to a single text. I plan on rectifying the not having her phone number issue tonight.

I park my car in the players' lot and head inside wearing one of my favorite suits. I had put it on earlier hoping that it would lighten my anger but it hasn't. In fact, my anger only grows as I walk inside the building the find Alyssa grinning at fucking Thorton. Again.

"Not fucking today." I growl to myself as I storm over to

Alyssa.

The grin on her face turns into shock and then fear as she takes me in.

"Hayes, what—" I shove Thorton out of the way, grab Alyssa by the upper arm and practically drag her into a closet, closing the door behind us and blocking her way out.

The fear that was once on her face has been replaced with fury. "Hayes, what the fuck are you doing? I have a job to do. One I can't do while locked in a closet."

"You've been avoiding me, Alyssa, and I don't fucking like it."

That's all it takes for shy Alyssa to come back. She shifts from one foot to the other, looking down. She mumbles something, but I can't hear it. It's too soft, too low.

"What?"

"I was fucking embarrassed." She says louder as she looks up at me, "I mean I fucking cried on you after we both... you know."

"Had mind-blowing orgasms?" I fill in for her.

Her cheeks turn pink. "Yes."

"That's nothing to be embarrassed about, baby. You were feeling a lot of emotions, and I'm pretty sure you may have been high off what you were feeling, and the orgasm had you crashing back down. It happens to a lot of people. Nothing to be embarrassed about."

"So it's happened to you before. A woman crying on your shoulder after an orgasm, then?"

I open my mouth to lie to her, but I can't. "No. It hasn't."

Her face falls, and she tries to move away from me, but I stop her, grabbing her by the shoulder and pulling her into me. She groans into my chest, and I smile as she grips my shirt. "I'm so embarrassed, Hayes." She whispers.

"Don't be, baby." I pull her head off my chest with my hands lightly on her cheeks so she can look at me. "If anything, I'm mad at you for running away after. I wanted to take care of you more."

She blinks up at me, confused. "You did?"

"Yeah, baby. I did." I admit softly as my thumbs brush her cheeks. "I wanted to make sure you were really okay. That what happened that night wasn't too much for you. Your first few times playing can be rough on your body and even more so on your mind. It killed me that you wouldn't let me check in with you."

Her eyes search my face as if she's trying to find the lie, but she won't. I mean every word.

"I'm sorry, Hayes."

"Just don't do it again, yeah?"

She bites her bottom lip, and I tug it from her teeth. "Yeah. Okay. I won't."

"Promise?"

"I promise."

"Good girl." I whisper, loving the way her eyes light up at my praise.

I lean down to kiss her when there's a bang at the door.

"Hayes, get out of the closet. It's time to gear up." Alyssa steps away from me, and I'm cursing Kolesnik for ruining the moment.

"You should go." She whispers. "Don't want to be late for your game and end up benched."

The thought of being benched makes me smirk. "Don't worry your pretty head about that, Alyssa. Coach would never bench me."

As much as I would like to pull her into me and kiss her, it's clear she's not in the place for that. She's slightly closed off, back in professional mode, and kissing her might just undo everything I have worked so hard on these last few weeks. I want to make her mine completely, I need it, but she isn't ready. Patience is key, and I have a ton of it.

"See you out there." I give her a wink before opening the door and finding Kolesnik on the other side waiting. "You want a turn now, Kolesnik? I have dick to spare."

Kolesnik slaps me on the back of the head before shoving me down the hallway. "Keep your dick to yourself, Hayes, no one wants it anyway."

"That's not what your mom was saying to me last night." I run down the hallway before he can slap me again and for the first time in a week I'm feeling good. My conversation with Alyssa went better than I hoped for and soon she'll be in my bed again, or at least my bed at the club until I can convince her she belongs in my actual bed. But that day is coming soon and I can't fucking wait.

Chapter 11

Alyssa

The next few weeks fly by in a blur of work and meeting Hayes at the club. It's honestly been amazing. Between the free use and exploring more with voyeurism and exhibitionism, my pussy has never been touched or fucked so much. And the aftercare and attention Hayes gives me afterwards is even better. I'm on a high right now. So high, in fact, that I made sweets for all the players because I couldn't go to bed after my night at the club. I was too awake.

As each player walks inside, I snap their picture and then hand them their goodie box. Each box is specialized to the players' likes—thankfully no allergies here.

I hand Kaprizov his box—triple chocolate brownies.

"For me?" he asks in his thick Russian accent.

I nod with a grin. "Yeah. They are brownies. I made everyone a small box of treats."

"Da?" he asks as he opens the lid and takes a sniff. "Chocolate chunk?" I nod. "They smell yummy. Thank you, Lyssa."

"You're welcome." I say as I turn back around to catch another player.

"You know. If we win tonight's game, you'll have to do this again, right?" Kolesnik says to me as he holds out his hand for his box.

I roll my eyes. "No, I won't. You guys have won many games without my treats. I doubt it'll change anything now."

"You say that. But this is it. If we win this game, we're in the playoffs. That changes things."

I shake my head. "No, that's—" The hair on the back of my neck stands on edge, and I swear I can feel fingertips running down my spine. Hayes is here, behind me somewhere. I'm sure of it.

"Is there a box for me, Alyssa?" He sounds almost jealous, and the way my name falls from his lips has me trying to hold back a shiver as his breath hits my ear.

"Yes," I whisper, trying my hardest not to moan. He hasn't even touched me, and yet I feel like I'm on the edge of an orgasm.

Without a thought, I lean over to grab his box from my bag on the floor, and then I feel it, his hard cock brushing against my ass. A gasp leaves my lips, and a bang from down the hall has me grabbing his box, straightening myself up, and taking a gigantic step away. "Here," I say, holding out his box of chocolate chunk peanut butter cookies.

The space I make for us is short-lived as he steps closer to me to grab his box. "If I didn't know any better, I'd say you were trying to make me jealous, Alyssa."

"What? I'm not—I don't—" his words have caused my brain to short-circuit. Jealous? Me? Him? No. That's… No.

He grins but there's a lustful look in his eyes as he stares at my reddening face. "No?" he questions.

I shake my head in reply, not trusting my voice.

"Hmmm," His eyes slowly move down and then up my body. My thighs clench together as my pussy lights up at his gaze. He gives me one last hungry look before he walks away, leaving me feeling like I just ran a marathon and with my panties soaking wet.

How is it that one human being can do things to my body the way he does? Seriously, all he did was look at me. Okay, and maybe he did brush his dick against my ass, but we were fully clothed, in public. He should not have so much control over me like that.

I do my best to continue my job—taking entrance pictures—while also giving out the rest of the treats to the players but Hayes and the hungry look he gave me is on my mind and I can't seem to muster up the same excitement that I had moments ago.

I'm gathering up my stuff so I can get ready to photograph the game when my phone goes off.

Hayes: Storage closet, 2 minutes.

He can't mean...

I shake my head and text back.

Alyssa: You're insane. No.

Hayes: 1 minute, Alyssa.

My heart races in my chest, and I look around the hallway, finding it mostly empty, except for Haylie.

She glances at my phone, and as she looks back at me, a grin spreads across her face. "You got time," she says before she walks away, not allowing me to respond.

My phone buzzes again.

Hayes: Now, Alyssa.

My feet move before I have even made up my mind. Of course I'm going to meet him in the storage closet, even if it's all kinds of wrong.

Hayes is already in there, dressed in his hockey gear, minus the skates, as I step inside.

He pushes me against the door, my bags dropping to the ground, and I almost care about the fact that I just dropped my very expensive camera onto the floor, almost.

"Do you have any idea what it's like for me to be in the locker room and hear what my teammates are saying about you?"

"What are they saying?" I ask, horrified. If any of them are making sexual comments I'm not sure I can live that down.

"They are all moaning over the desserts you made."

"They're just sweets." I whisper, taking in the hunger and anger on his face. My thighs rub together.

"They're your sweets, that you made with your own fucking hands, Alyssa. And all they can talk about is how amazing you are."

"It doesn't mean anything, Hayes. I just—"

"No one gets you but me, Alyssa. Not even those dicks at the club really get you."

"Hayes," I whisper, a mixture of scared and turned on. It's a weird combination to feel.

"Say it, Alyssa."

I lick my lips, debating on my next words, but the way he's looking at me has me saying, "No one but you, Hayes." His lips slam onto mine in a searing kiss, one I feel all the way down to my toes. He pulls away before I can slide my fingers into his hair.

"Meet me in the players' lot after the game."

My head is swimming, so all I can do is nod and agree, which makes Hayes grin and I feel even more gone for this man than I did just moments ago.

He carefully moves me to the side and then slips out the door. It takes me another few minutes to come back down to earth, and as I open the door, I can hear the excited screams coming from the bowl. The game is about to start and I'm not even at my post. Fuck.

Chapter 12

Oliver

The locker room is rowdy after our win tonight. Playoffs, here we come. Coach is going to put us through the wringer these next few weeks, and I plan on spending as much time between Alyssa's legs as I can tonight.

Fucking Alyssa.

Some of the guys are contributing her sweets to our win. Already talking about talking her into making some more. It's taking everything in me not to say anything because she's mine and they can't have her. Or her fucking sweets. Hockey superstition be damned.

I rush through my post-game cooldown, thankful I wasn't picked for press crap. The last thing I want to do is make Alyssa wait for me longer than necessary. But as I walk through the doors leading to the lot, I don't see her.

I try not to get too in my head over why and decide to wait for her. Leaning against the side of my car, my eyes trained on the doors. It's cold, but no colder than it was on the ice, so it doesn't bother me.

Every single time the door opens, I perk up just a little, but it isn't until Alyssa peeks her head out that a smile crosses my face.

She looks around tentatively, as if she's unsure. But the moment her eyes land on me, she smiles. It's barely there, but I see it. I see everything. Including the way she looks nervous as her gloved hand grips the strap of her camera bag while walking towards me.

"Hi," she whispers.

"Hi."

"I didn't think you'd still be here. They had me cover the pressroom tonight."

I shrug. "I waited." I wrap my arm around her shoulders and pull her towards the passenger side, opening the door for her so she can climb inside.

Alyssa is quiet as I get in the drivers' seat and start the car. She shivers in her coat as she stares out the windshield and I blast the heater to warm her up.

I pull out of the lot and start driving to Taco John's. I'm always starving after a game and there's nothing some good old Tex-Mex can't fix.

It doesn't take long to get there, and Alyssa stays quiet the whole time, which makes me nervous.

"What would you like?" I ask her as I pull up to the speaker box. She eyes the menu before asking for three steak tacos. I order her food plus mine and then some. There's no way she only eats three measly tacos, and there is no way I'm going to let her only eat that either.

The rest of the drive to my place is just as quiet, but I can't get myself to say anything. I want to know what's going on inside that head of hers, but I'm also worried if I pry, even just a little, she's going to run away.

Taking her home is new territory, one we haven't discussed, and I can only imagine how much she is freaking.

We walk inside the front door, and I toss my keys into the bowl on the table by the door before toeing my sneakers off and removing my coat and watching her do the same.

I grab her hand after hanging both coats on the wall hooks, walk her to the kitchen breakfast bar, and drop the three bags of food on the counter before pulling out a stool for her and waiting for her to sit.

"What are we doing, Hayes?" She asks, staring at the stool.

"Eating food."

Her eyes finally meet mine, and she looks so unsure. Of herself? Or me? I'm not sure. But what I do know is I hate it. "Yeah, but…" She looks around my place before looking back at me. "We don't meet outside the club and—"

"I want you, Alyssa." I say, cutting her off. "I have wanted you since the first moment I laid eyes on you and I've been moving slow. Trying to prove that I'm okay with the things you are into. That I'm into them too. Just in other ways. This is me trying to show you that you can have a committed relationship outside the club and still go to the club to be used. You can do that—have that. With me."

She stares at me, her mouth slightly open, her eyes wide with shock. "But… You…"

"I want to watch the excitement on your face while the people at the club use your body for their pleasure. Watch as your body shakes with every orgasm they pull out of you." Her thighs rub together and her breathing speeds up a touch. "All while knowing you and your pussy are mine."

She opens her mouth but I don't want to hear her reply. Can't risk the thought she might just say no, so I slam my lips onto hers and shove my tongue into her open mouth.

She stills for a moment before her fingers grip my shirt and her tongue moves against mine. My hands grip her hips and I move her backward until she's pressed up against the counter. Damn this high counter.

The soft whimper that leaves her throat has my dick pressing hard against the zipper of my jeans.

I break away from her lips, trailing open mouth kisses along her jaw and neck.

"Hayes," she moans, arching her neck and back to give me more access.

I run my tongue along the junction between her neck and shoulder before clasping down and sucking and nibbling. Fuck, her skin tastes so sweet.

The sound of her growling stomach has me freezing before I pop off her neck to find her face red from embarrassment.

"Oh my god," she whispers, covering her face with her hand.

I chuckle, and even through her embarrassment I can see the small smile on her face that she's trying to hide. Not wanting her to feel worse, I pull her into me, wrapping my arms around her.

"Come on," I say. "First, we'll eat tacos, and then I want your taco." Corney, I know. But I can feel her shaking in my arms from laughter, so it's totally worth it.

We sit at the counter, all the food I ordered open in front of us, and we eat. She ends up eating a side of rice and beans and five tacos, plus we share the chips and queso. I knew she could eat more than three tacos.

Alyssa helps me gather our trash and throw it away. Ready for her, I turn around and look at her. Her eyes widen as she takes me in and then takes a step back as I take one forward.

"Wait a minute," she says holding up her hands in an attempt to stop me from walking towards her. "We should talk about what you said. Before."

One step forward. One step backward.

"What's there to talk about, Alyssa? I told you what is happening. You and that pussy are mine now."

Forward.

Backward.

"And if I don't want to?" The corner of her mouth twitches, giving her away. She wants it. Wants me, and if she thinks she's going to get away with messing with me. Well, she's got the wrong guy.

Knowing she wants to be mine does things to my heart and cock, and I am definitely not playing her game tonight. Not after I opened up and told her what I wanted. What was going to happen between us.

I cross the room in three long strides, picking her up and tossing her over my shoulder. She squeals in delight.

"Tell me something, baby. Do you want my dick in your pussy or your mouth first?" Her thighs squeeze together and she whimpers.

She still hasn't answered by the time I reach my bedroom, but no matter, I'll pick for her.

Chapter 13

Alyssa

Tonight has been way more interesting than my mind could have ever conjured.

Hayes telling me he wants a relationship with me was not on my radar. Sure, the thought crossed my mind, but I quickly squashed it down. He never gave the impression that he wanted more than the fun we have at the club. And forget about me bringing it up. Especially after the first time where I basically avoided him like the plague after he had me say I was his so I could come.

Hayes slowly lowers me down to the floor of his bedroom. It's masculine in here, much like the rest of his home. Dark furniture, cream-colored walls and his room smells like him. Which is only making me crave him more.

"On your knees." He orders.

I drop to my knees quickly, hitting the carpet with a soft thud. I'm so ready for this I barely even register the pain from dropping so fast.

Without waiting another moment, I undo his pants, tugging

the top of his jeans and boxers down until his hard cock appears.

I waste no time wrapping my lips around his head and sucking.

"Fuck, Alyssa," Hayes grunts as his hand carefully, tenderly, lands on the top of my head.

The salty taste of his pre-cum hits my tongue, and I close my eyes as I moan. I have had many dicks in my mouth these last few weeks, but his is by far my favorite. The way it stretches around my lips, his taste. It does things to me no one else's does.

I move down his cock, taking him all the way to my throat before moving back up.

The sounds coming from Hayes as I move up and down his cock has my pussy crying for him. My panties are soaked.

Hayes' fingers thread through my hair, gripping the back of my skull before he starts moving my head up and down his cock. Tears fall from eyes as drool dribbles down my chin. It's messy and sounds wet, but I fucking love it. Crave it.

I look up at him to find him staring at me as he fucks my mouth. "Fuck, Alyssa, you look beautiful taking my cock down your throat."

I moan around his cock as he removes his cock from my mouth. "Fuck, baby, you can't do that. I almost blew my load and I want to do it in your pussy."

Grinning, I lick the drool and pre-cum from my lips. "Sorry." I say with a pant.

He leans over, placing a finger under my chin. "Don't ever apologize for that, baby."

Hayes slides his tongue inside my mouth kissing me. A whimper leaves my throat as I rub my thighs together.

"Do you need my cock in your pussy now?" he whispers against my lips.

"Yes. I need your cock. Please, Oliver." I beg.

His eyes turn dark and hungry. "Say that again." He growls.

"I need your cock."

"No. My name."

A small smile grows on my face. "Oliver."

He slams his lips to mine while he lifts me off the ground and carries me to his bed. Even as he lays me down and removes my jeans and panties, his lips never leave mine.

He slams his cock into me, and that's when our lips finally break. I practically scream as my pussy stretches around him. Pain and pleasure surge through my body with every thrust of his hips until all I feel is pleasure.

"Oh, fuck, Oliver." I moan, arching my chest.

"Again," he demands.

"Oliver." His name becomes a prayer on my lips as he fucks me.

He tugs my shirt and bra up, latching his mouth onto one of my nipples. Biting, sucking, teasing. The feeling goes straight to my pussy and my orgasm slams into me.

"This pussy was made for me and it's all fucking mine." He pulls away from my breast and straightens, his eyes cast down to where we meet, my legs spread wide. "Look at it, the way you just suck me back in."

I sit up on shaky elbows and look down, watching as he slides in and out.

His thumb brushes my clit once, twice. I throw my head back, moaning as my orgasm builds quickly. "Look at us, Alyssa."

My head snaps down, but watching the way his cock is covered in my release as it slides in and out of me and his thumb plays with my clit has my next orgasm on the rise. In a few more thrusts and a pinch to my clit I'm coming again.

Oliver doesn't let up; he keeps thrusting, keeps playing with my clit, and I can't stop coming. My legs quake as I come back to back to back. "Oliver, please," I cry out, begging him to stop and yet also begging for more. And more he gives.

"Oh, fuck, Alyssa. Yes. Fuck," he moans as he finally covers my walls with his release.

He grabs the back of my thighs as he pulls out of my pussy and watches as his cum slowly starts leaking out of me. "Damn, baby. You look so good covered in our mixed cum." He runs a finger up my slit and my body shivers as he shoves his cum back inside.

My pussy clenches around his fingers and he tuts. "What's the matter? Did my baby not come enough?"

"Oliver," I whine, my body exhausted. "No, I can't…"

"That's not what your pussy is saying," he says as he moves his fingers in and out of me slowly. "I think it needs to come one more time."

"Oli—" His name gets cut off with a moan as he moves faster, his thumb playing with my clit as he finger-fucks me.

My eyes fill with tears and his fingers move. "Oliver please. I can't. Please." My body feels like it's in overdrive and I try to move away from him, but I can't. My body won't let me, not really.

"Come on, baby, you can do it. Come for me. Come on my fingers."

My back arches off the bed, my toes curl, and my scream gets stuck in my throat as I come hard. Tears fall from my eyes as the orgasm takes over, and all I can feel and see is euphoria.

Oliver's arms are wrapped around me as I come back down to earth. His lips find purchase in every place he can reach while he whispers sweet nothings and praises. I wrap myself around him, needing to feel him against every part of my being. The only sounds in the room are from him; I'm still too lost in the haze to speak, so I just grip him close and nuzzle my face into his chest.

It isn't until I finally feel myself in my body that I realize I am speaking. But the only word coming from my lips is his name in a soft whisper. "Oliver. Oliver. Oliver."

"I'm here, baby. I got you." He whispers softly.

Even with my eyes closed, they still feel heavy, and I slowly drift off to sleep, still listening to the words Oliver whispers against my skin.

Chapter 14

Oliver

There is no greater feeling in the world than holding Alyssa in my arms. Not even the Stanley Cup we just won feels as amazing as she does.

My gaze finds hers on the ice as she lowers her camera from her face. Confetti rains down around us, and all I want is her.

I pass the cup to my teammate and head towards my girl, my woman, the love of my fucking life. The grin on her face slowly turns into shock, which I wipe off her face with a kiss.

The second my lips find hers, I wrap one arm around her back and grip the back of her head with my other hand, making sure she can't pull away from me.

This, her, right here in my arms, feels like home.

I can hear my teammates screaming and hollering all around us, cheering us on as I shove my tongue in her mouth so I can really taste her.

"Oliver, what are you doing? I thought we agreed." She whispers, her face turning beet red as I pull away.

"We did, and the cup is ours, so it is after."

After that night in my home, when I finally got her to be mine completely, we decided to keep our relationship between us until the season was over. She was worried it might complicate things if we announced our relationship before. Turns out, Alyssa is just as superstitious as most hockey players. So I agreed, albeit reluctantly, to keep our relationship a secret. But we just won the cup, the season is officially over, and I refuse to wait another minute to make sure everyone knows she's mine.

Shaking her head with a grin on her face, she buries her head into my chest as best she can with the padding on. "You're fucking insane, Oliver."

My arms tighten around her as the grin on my face spreads every more. "And yet, you love me all the same."

She looks up at me, her chin resting on my pads, and there's a sparkle in her eyes. "I do. I love you, Oliver, so fucking—"

My lips slam to hers once more, cutting her off. It's the first time she's admitted it to me. That she loves me. And hearing those words come from her lips has me feeling like I just saved the world from destruction.

The only thing that could make today even better would be if Alyssa told me she was carrying my baby. But I know she's still on birth control, and it's probably way too soon to be talking about babies, but I want them with her. I want the marriage, a dog, 2.5 kids, and a house with a porch, and I know we'll get there one day. But for now, I'm going to enjoy today because I won the Stanley Cup, and I got the girl I've always wanted to fall in love with me. What more could a guy ask for?

Freya's Other Works